For my father Robert Robert, who taught me how to build. – N.R.

www.enchantedlionbooks.com

First American edition published in 2014 by Enchanted Lion Books, 351 Van Brunt Street, Brooklyn, NY 11231
Copyright © 2012 for the illustrations by Geneviève Godbout
Copyright © 2012 for the text by Nadine Robert
Originally published in 2012 by Les Éditions de la Pastèque, Montréal, as *Joseph Fipps*.
Copyright © 2014 for the English-language text by Enchanted Lion Books
Translated from the French by Claudia Bedrick
All rights reserved under International and Pan-American Copyright Conventions
A CIP record is on file with the Library of Congress
ISBN: 978-1-59270-117-9. Printed in January 2014 by South China Printing Company

joseph Fipps

Nadine Robert
Geneviève Godbout

ENCHANTED LION BOOKS

NEW YORK

Again this morning Mommy called me Gremlin.
Every time I do something kind of silly, she calls me Gremlin.

So now my dad, my grandpa, and my grandma all call me
Gremlin, too. But Gremlin isn't my real name.

My name is Joseph Fipps!

I would like it a lot better if they called me Griffin.
The other day I saw a picture of this creature in a book.

It's an imaginary animal with the head and wings of
an eagle and the body of a lion.

Wow! If I were a griffin, I could fly all around in
the big blue sky.

But I'm not a griffin. I'm Joseph, I'm five years old,
and I live in a square house surrounded by five trees.

My favorite tree is the chestnut tree because
there's a goldfinch's nest hidden inside.

"Goldfinch" is a funny word to say.
This little bird is all yellow and lays light blue eggs.

Today I want to climb up to see if there are babies in the nest.
What if I borrow the ladder that's leaning against the house?

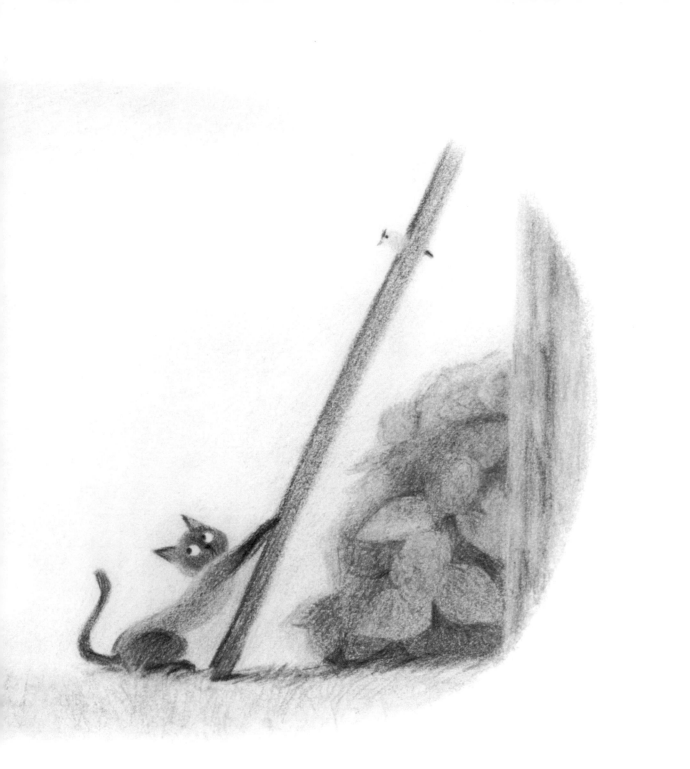

Standing straight up, the ladder will be taller
than the highest branch!

"Joseph!" Mommy is calling me.
"Leave that ladder alone and come inside right now!"

My mom saw me through the window.

Now I'm going to be scolded. Mommy's voice is always
different when she's angry!

As I go through the door, I say,
"I just wanted to see the nest!"

"I'm disappointed in you, my little gremlin.
You know you're too young to climb up
that ladder."

Ow, my ears! Then she says: "I've told you this a hundred times already. You never listen!"

Sometimes my mom gets all mixed up. Maybe she told me that two or three times. Now it's me who is really angry. If I had a griffin's wings, I'd fly far away.

I look at the floor. Then I blurt out:

"You always say 'no'! I can never do anything.
You're mean and I want another mommy."
She looks at me with big, round eyes.

But it's too late. I've said it.

"All right," she says, "I know a mommy who might be willing to have you. It's a walrus mommy and she lives on the banks of the North Pole. What do you think?"

I'm not sure if I've ever really seen a walrus or a walrus mommy.

All of a sudden I feel like I'm going to cry. When I think about the North Pole, my eyes begin to fill with tears.

I hope Mommy doesn't notice.

"You should think things over, Joseph. You want another Mommy and I've had just about enough of your silliness."

That's it! I run outside to sulk.

When I'm all filled up with feelings, I like to go to the banks
of the river that runs right by the chestnut tree.

I lie on my belly and look at the little waves
that ripple the water.

I wonder what it's like to live on ice. What does a walrus do all day? And how will I know which walrus is my mommy walrus?

If I were a griffin with my lion's fur, I'd never get cold.
If I were a griffin, I'd scare the polar bears with my pointy claws.

If I were a griffin…

"Hello, I've been waiting for you, little griffin," says an unfamiliar voice. Surprised, I look up and see an enormous animal.

Did I hear right? She called me Griffin!

I'm sooooo happy.

"Are you my new mommy?" I ask.

She doesn't answer but her big paw comes toward me. She's inviting me to climb up on her back. My heart is pounding but I'm not scared.

Mommy Walrus slides onto the ice. I laugh really
hard as we slip and slide and spin around in circles.
I don't fall off once!

I am Joseph the Griffin and I know how
to ride on a walrus's back!

Later she takes me to meet the baby walruses who are having
fun making holes in the ice with their tusks.

When the sun begins to set, Mommy Walrus says:

"If you'd like you can sleep here tonight. You don't need to be frightened."

Suddenly I feel cold. I don't have the fur of a griffin to keep me warm. And I don't have wings to fly home.

I'm Joseph, I'm five years old,
and I'm a little boy, not a griffin.

The funny thing is that I can hear
chirping and fluttering in my head.

I look around and Mommy Walrus is
no longer there. The ice is gone too!

Oh, my! I hear chirps from the
chestnut tree. It's the baby birds!

"Jooooseph!" Mommy is calling me.
"You've sulked enough. It's time to come inside."

What she doesn't know is that I've just come back from
the North Pole and I'm not sulking at all. I run to the house.

"Mommy! We have to go down to the ice banks together.
They're right near the river, behind the house. I want to
introduce you to Mommy Walrus. Come quickly!"

My mom doesn't understand a word I'm saying.
Her eyebrows are up really high and her mouth is open.

I don't know if Mommy's heart is beating as fast as mine.
What I know for sure is that I really did hear the baby birds
in the chestnut tree…

…but I haven't seen them yet!

The End